A Little Book of Folk Tales

Written by
Athey Thompson

A Little Book of folkTales

ISBN 978-1-7397800-29

Publisher. AThey Thompson

for sales information please Contact
email. AtheyThompson@yahoo.Com

Printed by. promising print Ltd
unit 51, LandyWood Enterprise park
Hollylane, great Wyrley, Staffordshire
Tel. 01543 577200

This edition printed in 2021, England

Contents

"O'er The Wild Ways
I Shall go
To Where Nature
Calls, And Soothes my Soul"

A faery Share

If ye Want to Welcome ye faeryfolk And invite them into your garden. Maybe you Shall Consider Leaving them a faery Share, A kind offering Left out at night, Shall always delight. Why. The faeryfolk Love homemade Bread and Butter, Now, that Would go down nicely Indeed. Or maybe Something Sweet, like Honey, they love honey. Or maybe a merry little Tipple of Whiskey or Mead. Ooh how merry they Shall be.

Always leave your offering With a kind heart, And only kind thoughts. And Maybe good Luck Shall Come your Way.

The Curious Tale about the faery Cobbler at the Inn in County Meath

A long time ago, fado fado, there be a Small Inn Which Was in a Village on the South Side of County Meath. TWas a busy little Inn Where travelling Wealthy men Would often Stay a night, Whilst travelling through Meath.

All Was fine until one day, the landlord Who be a miserable old fella, noticed a few Customers had Complained about missing Shoes.

Missing Shoes! I mean Who Would misplace their shoes, With Shoes being an expensive Luxury to have in those days.

Well, the landlord Wasn't too amused and he set about getting to the bottom of this Conundrum, So he did Sit up all night In one of the bedrooms Where reportedly Shoes had Vanished.

All Was quiet, that Was until 3.25 in the Morning. When a Scratching Noise Came from Inside the Wardrobe. All ears, the landlord Sat up on the bed and listened as the noise Continued.

With that, the Wardrobe door started to Creek open, Slowly as it did. And there stood In the Wardrobe, Would you believe, Was a Little faery man. Why, he must have been all of 3 foot tall, With beady eyes looking all around. He crept out of the Wardrobe, Right Into the glare of the landlord.

"Well now, Who the hell Will you be,
And What are ye doing
In my Wardrobe"

Yelled the landlord, As he stood up And looked down upon the Wee man.

Well, the little faery Man, he did not flinch as he stood afoot.

"Why, I be the local faery Cobbler, And I mends the faery Shoes, So I does"

Said the Wee man.

"Be damned if ye are, I tell ye to go away and never step a foot in my Inn again"

Yelled the landlord.

With that the Wee faery Cobbler turned back Into the Wardrobe and as he did, he muttered the Words

"Ooh ye Will be Sorry, I tell thee, Sorry Indeed"

from that day on, the Inn had nothing but bad luck. Ye faery Cobbler, he never returned. Although rumours of Shoes missing from a busy Inn on the North Side of County Meath did get about.

faery Rings

Theres Something Magical about a faery Ring. If you are lucky enough to See One, then you are truly blessed. However, Take heed as many a dark Tale has been told About faery Rings. We must be mindful of the Old folklores And Stay Well away, for No good Shall Come from entering a faery Ring.

Many Tell of folk Who have Vanished after Crossing a faery Ring, Only to return many years later, to find they have been gone for far too Long. Some Say folk have been Cursed upon for Interupting the fae As they danced upon their faery Ring. Be Well aware The fae Can be Mischievous And lure You Away.

The Month of May

As We Celebrate the Welcome arrival of Spring, We must remember, Tis the Month of May and the faery folk, oh they Love the month of May and they Shall be out and about Causing mischief and Mayhem Where ever they do go.

A tradition of May day eve, is to lay yellow flowers across your doorWay. or around your home, They Say this old Tradition keeps the faery folk aWay. As it is known that the faeries don't Like yellow flowers and they Shall not cross them. Many folk Lay Marigold or CoWslip, They even lay them over the entrance to CoWsheds or Barns to keep the Animals Safe.

Top of ye Well

In Ireland, Tis known for farmers to dread the eve of May day. Why, they Will Sit up all night Watching over their Water Well. for, they do Say, Tis bad luck if ye faery folk take the first drink of Water on Mayday Morn.

So farmers Will Keep Watch all evening ensuring they be the first to pour Water from their Well on the Morning of Mayday. Tis known as "Top of the Well" And it is Said, the first Water of Mayday Must be Saved and Kept Safe for the year ahead. This Old tradition Brings good luck and good health & protection for the farmer And his family And farm Animals.

"To See the Beauty
Within a dew drop
That has fallen upon a leaf
is to See the Wonders
of the World"

Tale of the young girl Who took
Water from a faery Wishing Well.

There be a fairtale I must tell ye
far far away in the Woods of County
Wicklow, In that there Cottage
Lives an old lady, Who is Well known
to have the healing hands. upon one
darkened night over the Month of May
A visitor Came a Calling.

A tap, tap, tap, tap,
goes the front door.
Why, Who be knocking upon my door
This late at night
Wonders the Old lady.

Tis a young girl, Who stands outside, All alone she has lost her Way. And Shes Lost in a faery Stray. The old Lady, She knows of Such a Look, So She brings the young girl inside and a Seat by the fire She took.

"Now child, tell me, What you be doing out this time of night, All alone, When All around is a fright, These parts, Why They be no good. Tis no place for a Little girl"

Asked the old Lady.

The little girl tells how She found herself to be lost and Confused, So When she Came upon a Watering Well, She helped herself to a drink of Water. And Since Then she has felt unWell.

"Ooh child, What a thing to do,
I Say, What a thing to do.
Why, that Watering Well, it be a faery Wishing Well, its Water is only for the faery folk. And there be a Stray Cursed upon anyone Who drinks its Water.
But, not to Worry child, I know of a Cure."
"Now let me See"
Said the old lady.
The healer turns to her basket of healing Potions and places onto her table.
A muttering And A mumbling as She does, She takes herbs and mixes it With a green potion in a bowl, She adds Mouldy old mushrooms and moss. She then pours The Lumpy green mixture into an old Large feeding bucket.

"There now child, Take off ye shoes and Stand barefooted in this there bucket.
And here you'll Stand until 3 minutes Past the 3 of clock"
Tells the healer.

So be it, there she stood still in the bucket And as the clock passed 3 minutes of the 3 of clock, the little girl felt a strong rush of Wind go around her, and it left by the front door. The old lady heard the door Rattle, And she knew the stray Was gone and a good riddance!

After a few hours rest, a bowl of food and a drink of milk, the little girl Set off home,

Never to be Seen in those parts ever again.

ye faeryfort

Look up high, Look down Low for hidden between the rugged old hills. And ye grassy Wild meadows is a fuerjfort. Why. Many may be found upon farm Land Where Cattle graze and folk do dwell.

Tis a fuery fort
Thats What I thought
O, but be aware
I Wouldn't dare
go messing around
upon Such a Mound.

They do Say a fuery fort, a Rath
is the home of ye gentlefolk,
the goodfolk they be.

Tis known to be a gateway to the other Worlds, the elemental Worlds, Where the others do dwell. Theres a fine veil between our Worlds. And Sometimes if you are Lucky, ye may Just Catch a glimpse.

In Ireland, faeryforts are protected And in general Looked upon with great Respect. You'll not find an Irish man messing with a faery fort. These forts Be ancient, So if you Come across one Be gentle, be kind and keep in mind "A faery may be Near."

To believe or not to believe, that is your choice, But as an Irish man once Said, "I don't believe in faeries, but I know they are there."

The Tale of the odd happenings At young Marys farm in Tipperary

The old Lady, Who lives down the Way
O'er there, She told me this tale one day.

There once lived a fair young Maid, called Mary, Who did live alone on a Small farm in Tipperary. She kept a few dairy Cows that gave great milk, And With this fine milk She Made the bestest butter in all of Tipperary. Why this butter made her enough Money to get by.

On her farmland Was a row of Old Apple Trees. Why these old Apple Trees grew the Most delicious big Apples. And in the Autumn Months Mary Would gather them up, And bake the Most tastiest Apple pies.

Young Mary Would Sell a Cart full of Apple pies every Week at the local farmers market, So things Were going nicely for young Mary.

But all Was about to take an odd turn, T'Was during a Very Wet and damp Autumn that Strange things did start to happen.

One morning baskets full of freshly Picked Apples did mary find Waiting upon her doorstep, Another Morning She found a full bucket of freshly pulled milk.

Well, this Was all peculiar and Worried Poor Mary, So oneday Whilst at the farmers Market She Came upon the local healer Lady. And Mary told her of the oddities happening at her farm.

The healer told Mary to leave 3 Cups of fresh milk and 3 bowls of stew out on the kitchen table for 12 at night.

So that very night Mary did as the healer told, And as the clock turned to 12 at night, Mary Crept down the stairs and Slowly opened the kitchen door.

And there Sat at the kitchen table, she found 3 little Elves, Oh they Were eating and drinking and having a Merry old time.

Turns out the 3 elves had felt the Cold and took to resting in Marys barn. They took a Shine to lonesome young Mary.

So In return for a Warm dry resting place, they took to helping Mary With her chores.

As the Story goes, they brought great Luck to Mary, And they Stayed for a long time.

Jack O Lantern

Oh, he be a beast of a little man
That Stingy old Jack O Lantern, forever he Will
Be a lost Soul as he Wanders the Realms of
No Mans Land.
Neither heaven nor hell Would let him in.
Why, even the faeryfolk turned him aWay.
O, he thought he Could fool the devil
And a fool he be to think So.

O, here he be
There he be
Wandering free

O, here he be
There he be
Looking for thee

O, here he be
There he be
Trouble is he
O, here he be
There he be
Just Wait and See

Over all hallows eve, they do say
That wicked Old Jack wanders the land.

Many years ago in Ireland, Over All Hallows eve it was tradition to carve out ugly faces onto lumpy old Turnips or Potatoes and place them onto window sills, Believing that this would frighten off Old Jack or any other nasty Spirits that be wandering around.

Over the years the tradition travelled to other Countrys, where pumpkins were used instead of Turnips.

When ye faery folk Come

When they do Come, from neath an
earthy mound, They do Come.
O'er from meadows deep
When they do Come, There be no Sound
They Come to forage, and to eat.
If ye be kind enough to leave
A Share, it Shall be known
of butter, cheese or milk
Left outside, upon the ground
And When they do Come. At night
it Shall be found.
And the passers by. Who pass by
Shall bless you in return
And leave you
Well alone.

Down the Old Corpse Road

Let me tell you of ye Old Corpse road or
churchway as it be Called. Tis a pathway
that Was used many a year ago,
Tis Where the poor old Souls Were Carried
In Coffins, over many fields and pathways
for miles and miles. Slowly Carried towards
the nearest church, Where they Would be
Buried and finally laid to rest
And most times, Twas in the dark.

Although these Old pathways have
Long gone by, Some are Still used as paths
And it be known that the poor spirits
of those Carried upon it, still linger
for they shalt not rest.

if you ever Come across a field that is named Church-Way or kirk-Way, then Many a year ago, that field Was crossed by a church Way path. You may feel uneasy In these fields, Some Say these fields be nothing but bad luck, and No good Shall Come of them.

Over the Old Corpse Ways, they Say you may find the hungry grass. In Ireland its Called the fear gortach. Tradition Says the hungry grass grows in Such places Where a Coffin Was laid down during its Journey to a church, And there the Sad Soul Seeped out of the Coffin and into the ground.

If you happen to bread upon the hungry grass then a desperate hunger Shall overWhelm you, So much So that in Such a place in

 Ballinamore a local lady keeps food ready.

Ready, for anyone Who has treaded upon the hungry grass and fell into Such a desperate hunger.

Some Say the hungry grass does Come from the fuery folk. They Say the fueries felt Such an overWhelming Sadness as they Watched the Suffering of the hungry. So they Cast a spell of Anger, A desperate hunger to anyone Who treaded upon its ground.

Along Some old church pathWays, Coffin stones or Corpse stones Were Laid, So a Coffin Could be rested down for a While, So the Carriers Could Rest. You may Still See these Old Stones along these old paths. They Say these Old Stones are haunted by the old Souls, the dead Souls of times gone by.

O'er there
Is Where We Shall go
And go, Shall We
for hidden a Way
far, far, a Way
A faery once did Say
Betwixt ye Trees
Betwixt ye branches
Betwixt ye Leaves
Is Where We do Meet
Is Where We do Wait
ye See
And, if ye Shall pass on by
If ye might
Stand neath an Olden Tree
And take a Sip, from a dew drop
upon a leaf
Well ye Might Just See, So O'er there
We Shall go, And go Shall We....

A changeling Cometh

There be many an old Tale told
About ye good folk, ye kind folk, ye faery folk.
Oh Why they Can be good And they Can be
kind, that much is true, but We ought
Remember, There be a dark Side to ye fae.

A mother does Cry out
upon the darkest of hour
for her child has gone
Been taken away
And there Laying in its crib
There be a changeling
Oh it be a Whining, Withered, Wretched
old thing, Cast away from its own
No good Shall Come from it
for it shall never rest

As the Old tales Were told,
A new mother Would Come to find her
Newborn or infant child had changed.
As if over night, for Some the
childs Looks had gone, gone aWay
And the child Was acting Odd.
The poor mother Would be left brokenhearted.
for She Would fear, A changeling.
Sure enough, the faery folk had Called
upon this New mothers home and they had
taken aWay her beautiful child, and left
In its place an unWanted one, a beast of a
faery that had been Cast aWay.
In most Cases the changeling Would
Never rest, it be a nasty beast. for Some, the
faeries took pity and returned the human
child, or Some mothers Sought help from the
healing Ones.

The Tale of the pooka upon a gentle path.

Somewhere in County kerry, over that hill And around about that Way. There be a gentle path. It's a long and Winding path that no one ever dares to Walk upon.

Thats Right, It be known as the faery Way. Tis a faery path and is best left Well Alone.

Well this old tale be about two young fellas from the local village, Who thought they knew best, they thought that the faeries, Well they didn't exist.

So upon one night, After a few too many pints they thought it be funny to Walk A different Way home. Why, foolish & drunk they headed straight for the faery Way.

It had turned past 12 midnight by now, And all around Was pitch dark, and it Was Raining as the two fellas made their Way. upon entering onto the fair path, they Let out loud Laughs and pushed eachother on as they Walked further on down the path.

Meeting about the half Way Mark, they hear a horse galloping, then out of the darkness they See a horse heading up the PathWay. Its galloping at such a speed, Why as it passes them they have to jump from the pathWay, over a Stone Wall they go, into a field, landing in a pile of horse manure as they does. As they both Clamber to Stand up, they be Covered in horse Manure.

With that; the horse turns around and Comes back toWards them, as it nears they hear A voice, Which does Say.

"What ye lads be doing upon my path"

Peeking over the StoneWall, petrified, the two fellas Say not a Word as they See infront, the biggest horse they have ever seen, Why this mighty beast, must be 8 foot tall ! and on Top theres a Wee man, he's holding a torch out on a long stick, And he doesn't look to pleased.

he does Say out load, "Ye lads be told, If ye ever dare to tread upon my path Way again Well I be Waiting fur ye"

And With that the horse races off back down The path.

The two fellas, Covered in Manure, Stumble back home across the Wet and darkened fields. Where the mud Was So thick they lost their Shoes. Some do Say, the two fellas got lost in the fear And Wandered the Wet Cold fields all night.

Toadstools in the Woodlands

Toadstools, O they love the damp Soggy ground of Autumn. They flourish upon mossy Covered fallen Tree Trunks, or Tall grassy patches. They nestle neath Woodland ferns, often they be hiding away, hoping to stay for another day.

Be gentle as you Walk upon the fallen Autumn Leaves, as there may be Magical toadstools neath those very leaves.

They do Say, you must never go eating these magical Toadstools. for, they be trouble, they may take ye far far away, into a stray.

O, did ye Come to See
A Toadstool or tWo or three
Why, tread Softly must ye
for hiding underneath
A faery There Shall be.

Why the faeryfolk, they love Toadstools
Whether they be red With Spots or BroWn
With Wrinkled Soggy flat tops. Many a
time A faery has been Seen dancing
Around a toadstool.
The old tales do tell, if We ever Come
upon a Circle of mushrooms, Well that be
the faeries Ring, So leave it Well alone.
Don't go Crossing it, or Standing in it,
Oh no, for this Will anger the faeryfolk
They May Just Cast a Nasty Spell upon ye.

Ye faery Tree

If ye take to Walking upon the fine Spring meadows or hills during the Month of May, you May be Sure to Come across the lone hawthorn tree, And in Bloom it Shall be.

for they do have the Most beautiful delicate pretty petals in bunches of Bloom.

Such a Sight to See, Why, you Cannot help but take a closer Look, but be told my dear, these blooms are not for Picking, for hidden upon its Branches Are Sharp Thorns So be Warned.

With a twisted old trunk Covered
In lichen and moss and a gnarled bark.
Often the bough of the tree arches over
to Create What Looks Like a doorWay.
An entrance to the other Worlds.
for the old folklores do tell, that
Beneath the hawthorn Tree is Where
the fair folk do dwell, This be
A faery Tree.

So if you do Come upon Such a Tree
And ye Wonder of its Secrets.
Be Sure to remember, tis the home
of the faery folk, So be respectful
be kind, And mind
how you go.

Who are they

Why, Who are they
These gentlefolk, that they talk about
The others as they be known
Why Could they be nothing More
Than an evening filled With too much Ale
And a darkened Late night Walk home
or, maybe not, Just mind
They be true
Those Olden Tales told many a year
About them
How they be O'er the Way, O'er there
All alone
Where the Woods be deep
Where the hills be high
And, Where the glens be Wild

They do Say
In those Such places
If ye shall Come
upon a Lone hawthorn Tree
Stood upon the foot of a hill
Why,
They do Say, this be Where they dwell
The gentle folk, the good folk
The faery folk they be.
Now,
Whether they be there
Or, Whether they not be there
Tis not for me to Say
Nor is it for you.

I'm over the Moon
That you have purchased
One of my Little Books
Thankyou.

My Little Books Available
A Little Book of Poetry
A Little Book of faery Tales
A Little Book of folk Tales

You May follow me

facebook · Tales of the old forest faeries
Instagram · Athey · Thompson